SCOOBY-DOO!
SHIVER ME TIMBERS

by Sonia Sander Illustrated by Scott Gross Book design by John Sazaklis

ABDOPUBLISHING.COM

Reinforced library bound edition published in 2016 by Spotlight, a division of ABDO. PO Box 398166, Minneapolis, Minnesota 55439.
Spotlight produces high-quality reinforced library bound editions for schools and libraries. Published by agreement with Warner Bros. Entertainment Inc.

Printed in the United States of America, North Mankato, Minnesota.
092015   012016

THIS BOOK CONTAINS
RECYCLED MATERIALS

CATALOGING-IN-PUBLICATION DATA

Sander, Sonia.
 Scooby-Doo in shiver me timbers / Sonia Sander.
   p. cm. (Scooby-Doo)
Summary: Some pirate ghosts are putting an even scarier take on a haunted pirate show. Can Mystery, Inc.
solve the mystery before the curtain drops?
1. Scooby-Doo (Fictitious character)--Juvenile fiction. 2. Dogs--Juvenile fiction. 3. Ghosts--Juvenile fiction.
4. Pirates--Juvenile fiction. 5. Mystery and detective stories--Juvenile fiction. 6. Adventure and adventures
--Juvenile fiction.
[E]--dc23

                2015156070

978-1-61479-408-0   (Reinforced Library Bound Edition)

SHIVER ME TIMBERS

A HAUNTED PIRATE SHOW

The gang was on their way back to Coolsville.

"Like, are we there yet?" asked Shaggy.

"If the weather doesn't get worse, we'll be home in an hour," said Fred.

Just then the Mystery Machine sputtered to a stop.

"Jinkies!" said Velma. "That didn't sound good."

"Engine trouble," Fred said as he checked under the hood.
"Jeepers!" said Daphne, as the rain poured down harder.
"Let's get out of the rain and find some help."

There was an old fort along the road. The gang climbed the hill to the front door. "Like, it doesn't look like anyone's home," said Shaggy.

Suddenly, the door swung open, revealing a mummy and a ghoul.
"Zoinks!" cried Shaggy. "This place keeps getting creepier!"
Shaggy and Scooby tried to run. But the monsters were only actors.
"So sorry we scared you," said the owner, Julian. "Ava and I just
finished up our show."

Julian invited the gang inside.
"What is this place?" asked Fred.
"It's an old pirate fort," said Julian. "We use it for our haunted pirate show."
"Only lately," said Ava, "real pirate ghosts have been scaring away our audience."
"They've even scared away most of my actors," Julian added. "Maya and Marcus are the only ones who've stayed."

The gang offered to help with the show and solve the mystery.

Ava and Maya found the gang some costumes.

"Like, ahoy matey!" said Shaggy.

"R'ahoy!" said Scooby.

That night, the gang took their places on stage.

"Beware the pirate curse if you steal our treasure," said Fred.

Julian and Ava jumped out and scared the crowd.

All of a sudden, a thick cloud of smoke filled the fort.

"Avast ye who dare to trespass, dead men tell no tales!" said a creepy pirate ghost.

The audience fled as fast as they could.

Then, the lights went out and the ghosts let out a chilling laugh.

"Trespassers beware!" the ghosts howled as they chased after the gang.

"Like, we should have left when we had the chance!" cried Shaggy.

"Quick! Hide in there," said Velma, pointing to a nearby door.

The gang quickly hid in a supply room.
"It looks like we lost the ghosts," said Fred.
With the coast clear, the gang took a look around.

Shaggy and Scooby started to play with the swords.

Scooby got his sword stuck in the wall. When he pulled the sword out, he opened a hidden door.

Behind the door was a secret tunnel.

"Let's take a look," said Fred.

"Like, maybe that door was hidden for a reason," said Shaggy.

"There's nothing down here but dust and spiders," said Velma.

"Riders?" said Scooby. "Rikes!"

"Jeepers!" said Daphne. "Look at this shiny gold coin!"

"It must be a fake coin from the show," said Fred.

"It looks pretty real to me," said Velma. "We can ask Julian about it."

"First let's see what's at the end of the tunnel," said Fred.
"I was afraid he was going to say that," said Shaggy.
The only thing at the end of the tunnel was the outside.
But Fred saw a flashing light. "It looks like a signal is being sent from that tower," he said.

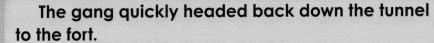

The gang quickly headed back down the tunnel to the fort.

At the door they spotted a dark figure in a pirate hat stuffing a cannon with a piece of paper.

"That pirate looks awfully suspicious," said Velma.

"I wonder what he's up to?" asked Daphne.

After the mysterious pirate left, the gang took a closer look.

"Like, it's just a map of the fort," said Shaggy.

"This is not just any map," said Velma. "It looks like someone is searching for something."

At dinner, Fred showed the gold coin to Julian.

"Where do you think it came from?" asked Fred.

"There's a legend that says a group of pirates robbed a ship and hid the coins in this fort," explained Julian.

"And if anyone ever tries to claim the coins, they will be cursed forever."

Later the gang went up to the tower to look for clues.
"Look!" said Fred. "The ghost left behind its flashlight."
"I wonder who they're sending messages to," said Velma.
"Like, what if whoever they were signaling is watching us?" asked Shaggy.

Suddenly, the pirate ghosts burst onto the tower.

"Zoinks!" cried Shaggy. "Like, I knew we were being watched!"

"Run!" yelled Scooby.

The ghosts chased Scooby and the gang down the winding stairs.

"Like, these stairs are making me dizzy!" cried Shaggy.

"There must be a place to hide at
the bottom," said Fred.
   But there wasn't anywhere to hide.
There was only a long hallway.
   The gang ran down the hallway and
fell through a trapdoor.
   "Ruh-roh!" cried Scooby.

"Like, at least we got rid of those frightening freaks," said Shaggy.

"But where are we now?" asked Daphne.

"Jinkies!" said Velma. "This is where they run the show's smoke machine."

"Hmm. . . that gives me an idea. Maybe we can smoke out the ghosts once and for all," said Fred.

Before the start of the next show, Fred set up the smoke machine.
"Now all we need to do is shoot the cannon and scare the ghosts into falling into the trapdoor," said Fred.
"Shaggy and Scooby, are you ready to light the cannons?"
"Aye, aye, captain," said Shaggy.

Just as they hoped, the pirate ghosts tried to stop the show.

But this time the gang wasn't going to let them.

Just as the ghosts burst onto the stage, Shaggy and Scooby fired the cannons.

The stage shook with each blast. The ghosts were so scared they stopped in their tracks.

As the cannon fired again, they both backed up and fell through the trapdoor.

"Trespassers beware!" said Daphne, as she closed and locked the door.

The audience cheered. "That was the best show ever," they cried.

Once the audience was gone, the gang unmasked the trapped ghosts.

It was Maya and Marcus.

"We were so close to finding the gold," said Maya.

"We would have, too, if it weren't for you meddling kids!" said Marcus.

The next day, the gang got ready to go home.

"I'm so glad your van broke down here," said Julian. "You not only saved my show, you made it better!"

Back home, Scooby and the gang unloaded the Mystery Machine.
"It was nice of Julian to let us keep our costumes," said Daphne.
"These will be great for next Halloween!"
"Scooby-Dooby-Doo!"